My Three Days in Gilead

Elmer Ulysses Hoenshal

Contents

MY THREE DAYS IN GILEAD

BY

Elmer Ulysses Hoenshal

My Three Days in Gilead

I love to breathe where Gilead sheds her balm;
I love to walk on Jordan's banks of palm;
I love to wet my foot in Herman's dews;
I love the promptings of Isaiah's muse;
In Carmel's holy grots I'll court repose,
And deck my mossy couch with Sharon's deathless rose.

--J. PIERPONT.

MY THREE DAYS IN GILEAD
By Elmer U. Hoenshel, D. D.,

Principal of Shenandoah Collegiate Institute and School of Music

In profound gratitude, this little volume is dedicated to the memory of William Barakat of Jerusalem.

My faithful, careful dragoman, who in manhood's prime, yet not many months before his death, guided me in safety, not only during my trying "Three Days in Gilead," but also throughout an extended tour otherwhere in his native land--the Holy Land of my faith.

THE AUTHOR

INTRODUCTION

At last, after waiting twenty leaden-winged years from the time in which a fixed purpose was formed in me to visit the Orient, the realization came. The year that saw the fulfillment of my cherished ambition was definitely determined upon eight summers before it took its place in the calendar of history. Fortune smiled upon my plan. I was ready. My joy was akin to ecstasy.

Imagine my disappointment when, in the month of May of my chosen year, 1900, I learned that no agency would organize a tourist party to move at a time in the summer or autumn that would suit me! There was but one alternative--to travel independent of any organization. This I would do. The decision to do so brought instant and happy relief.

At no time in my period of absence of five months did I meet a single former acquaintance. I planned every move, and held myself in every way responsible for results. The experience I thus gained in the many countries visited I value highly. Not infrequently I found myself in trying situations; but all ended well. To-day, in my inventory of life's rich and helpful experiences, though it were possible for me to do it, I would not eliminate one of these. It was a kind Providence that denied me the luxury of a place in a modern "personally conducted" tourist party.

A few articles descriptive of certain experiences have been written by me for publication. Some themes I have presented on the lecture platform a few hundred times. My auditors, universally, have been kind in their criticisms. Many have been the requests that I write a volume reciting the story of my travels. In response I have steadily refused. Many books on travel have appeared in recent years, possibly too many; but I have seen very little that has been written about the trans-Jordanic highlands. And it is not strange, for, though multitudes of tourists annually visit

Palestine, not one person out of a thousand of them ever goes east of the Jordan. And is it worth while? We shall see.

On my trip I tried to identify no biblical site; I tried to locate no city of antiquity; I dug into no mound; I disturbed no ruin. All this I left to the geographer, the historian, and the archaeologist who had preceded me, or who should come after me. True, with the help of my Bible, map, guide-book, and guide, I formed opinions, and was happy in the fitness of some of them; but, in the main, I was content to rest in the conclusions reached by those who had studied scientifically and reverently every hill and valley and ruin in this neglected region.

But my observation and experience no other has had. I know of no other who mapped out or traveled the route chosen by me. I sought and expected much; I found and experienced more. And though eight years have passed since my journeyings in Gilead, yet so fresh is the memory of those days that I need make but slight reference, as I write, to the notes that were then written. Often, in recent years, I have found myself lingering in thought on some high ridge looking out over an extended panorama filled with sacred associations, or silently gazing up into the strangely impressive Oriental sky by night. Even as I write I seem to catch again a perfume-laden breeze, bearing repose to my weary soul. And if the memory of this land seen in its desolation is so refreshing to a foreigner, what must not the possession of the real in the days of its fatness have been to the weary, battle-scarred Israelites who secured permission to abide here!

So, in response to the call of my friends, and with the hope of adding somewhat to the meager fund of information concerning a once famous district, or, at least, to create additional interest in the territory occupied by the tribe of Gad in the days of early allotment, I undertake to tell the story of "My Three Days in Gilead."

Dayton, Virginia, February 20, 1909.

"Waiting at Damascus"
CHAPTER I.

Damascus! A city that numbers the years of its existence in millenniums; that witnessed in the dawn of history the migration of Abraham as he went out from Ur to a land not known to him, and to whom she gave one of the best of her sons; that sent out the leper, Naaman, to Palestine for healing and received him back whole; that hailed with great preparations the coming of Elisha, who had previously blinded her army at Dothan; that welcomed Saul of Tarsus in his blindness, restored his sight, and sent him, transformed in his life, to transform Asia Minor and classic Europe. Damascus! A city surviving an age-long struggle with the encroaching desert--a struggle that must go on through ages to come; but, as long as the Abana and Pharpar continue to flow, the sands that would bury her forever in oblivion will be changed into a soil of life-giving and life-sustaining fertility sufficient to support her thousands of inhabitants. Damascus! A city of the long ago, practically unchanged, where the Occidental may look to-day with unfeigned interest upon architecture, costumes, and customs similar to those that prevailed in the East while Greece and Rome were yet young. Damascus! A city celebrated for a thousand years for its bazaars, work-shops, and roses; a city so beautiful thirteen hundred years ago that Mohammed, viewing it for the first time from a distance, is said to have exclaimed: "Man can have but one paradise. My paradise is heaven; I cannot enter yonder city!" a city to-day of unsurpassed beauty, when viewed from the distance, with its white domes and slender minarets rising above the shrubbery and trees of its thirty thousand gardens. Here in this old city; in this historic city; in this beautiful city; in Damascus, I greet you and extend to you an invitation to join me in my proposed trip through Gilead.

My party as yet consists of but two persons. My dragoman, William Barakat, of

Jerusalem, in response to a telegram sent from Constantinople, met me several days ago at Beyrout. He is a native Syrian, talks good English, dresses like an American, (save that he wears a red fez,) and is a Christian in faith. Before reaching this city he has already rendered me excellent service. He is intelligent, having attended the American College at Beyrout. I can trust him.

My arrangements with my guide are simple. He is to take me over my desired route by best possible methods of travel; to furnish the best of fare and lodging obtainable; to guarantee me a safe escort; and he is to do all this within a specified time and for a stipulated price. I did not then know how little I was asking as to fare and lodging, but when I knew that he was fulfilling his part of the agreement I had little cause for just complaint.

By early dawn, on October thirtieth, we had breakfasted and had bidden good-by to all the servants about the hotel, (many of whom I did not know to exist, but who, somehow, had learned of me, and had risen thus early to witness my departure and to ask a fee for services that I am quite sure some of them had had no part in rendering,) and had ordered the driver to lose no time in reaching the station of the Damascus-Hauran Railroad, about two miles distant. But, notwithstanding the early hour, the streets were already crowded with people, mules, donkeys, dogs, and other things. It was only with great effort that we could make any headway, and at times it seemed that the crowd, angered at our persistence, would stop us entirely in our struggle to pass through. We did the best we could, but we missed the train. Since there were ONLY THREE TRAINS A WEEK on that road, it meant that I must go back to that same hotel and spend two more days in Damascus at the rate of ten dollars a day, and then, again, on leaving, must fee those same servants for service that I did not want, and, generally speaking, did not get. But, though the disappointment was great, it brought additional opportunity to study the wonders and ways of the wonderful city wherein I was forced to remain.

A second time my dragoman prepares food for our journey; and again, on the morning of November first, we hurry to the station. This time we do not miss the train--we wait for it--and we wait a long time; but with the waiting there is contentment, for, if the train move south, I, too, am sure of going.

"Through Bashan"
CHAPTER II.

At the time of this writing there is a railroad extending from Damascus to Mecca, but at the time of my visit the terminus was at Mezarib, a small town about fifty miles south of Damascus, near the northern boundary-line of Gilead. It was in my plan to travel that distance by rail; hence my presence at the city railroad station.

The ride to Mezarib, through Bashan, especially that part of it now known as the Hauran, is one of more than ordinary interest. For the first twenty-five miles the land is literally covered with black basaltic rocks, as is also part of the remaining distance. How it is cultivated I can scarcely understand, for I am sure that the American horse could not be made to serve well here. But I was told that the natives do cultivate it, and that they raise excellent crops of grain. When I looked upon them at work with their crude wooden plows and brush harrows, and then heard that they raise excellent crops of grain, I was satisfied that the land must be very fertile; and I was reminded of a certain humorist's remark about the fertility of some land in Kansas, of which he said, "All you need to do is to tickle the ground with a hoe, and it will laugh with a big harvest." Farther on the rocks almost entirely disappear, and there is spread out a beautiful valley, extending far to the south, whose fertility and pasturage attracted the Israelites on their march to Canaan, and which, ever since, has caused the name "Bashan" to be a synonym for "plenty." And, because of its abundant production of grain, which finds a ready market in Damascus, it has been aptly called the "granary of Damascus."

The manner in which this grain is put on the market is quite novel to me. I see hundreds of camels loaded with large sacks of grain moving with slow, swinging tread toward Damascus, or returning unloaded to the desert. The camels proceed in single file, usually ten or more in a train, and each is led by means of a rope fastened to the animal next in front--the rope of the foremost of all being fastened to the saddle of a donkey, on which the owner, or driver, usually rides. Many grindstones also are shipped from this country, one large stone constituting a load for a camel. This land is, also a great grazing region, and for more than three thousand years Bashan has been celebrated for its fine breed of cattle.

Some distance south of Damascus I cross the headwaters of the Pharpar River, whose clear, sparkling water Naaman considered much more suitable for a general's bath than the muddy water of the Jordan. At my place of crossing an athlete could clear the stream at a single bound.

The distant scenery deserves more than a passing notice, though but little more can be given here. Off to the west, in plain view, is Mount Hermon, whose towering, snow-capped summit in all probability looked upon the transfigured person of the Son of Man. To the east is the Lejah, in, or near which is Edrei, where Og, the giant king of Bashan, was slain in the attempt to hold his realm against the home-seeking Israelites under the leadership of Moses. South of the Lejah are the Hauran Mountains, now occupied by the Druses, a people of a peculiar religious faith--a faith which is a mixture of Mohammedan, Christian, and Zoroastrian elements. One of their beliefs is that the number of souls in existence never varies. "Accordingly, all the souls now in life have lived in some human form since the creation, and will continue to live till the final destruction of the world." To them prayer is thought to be an unwarrantable interference with the Almighty. They, having colonized this mountain, are at present causing the Turkish government much trouble. They number about 90,000, and are almost continuously at war with the neighboring Bedouin tribes. And because of the feuds which prevail here, it is expected, and I believe is a matter of law, that all visitors to this region must have an escort either of soldiers or Bedouins. Were not robbery and bloodshed so prevalent in the East-Jordan country, its ruins and scenery would attract hundreds of tourists where now but a few ever suffer their curiosity or interest in Bible lands to turn them aside from the beaten paths of travel. In my course I pass through a portion of the land of which we read in Deut. 3:3-5, noted for its many "rock cities." I look upon the ruins of a number of these, but have little opportunity for a close examination. The most noted ruins that I see are at Sunamein and at Mezarib. But those who have pressed farther east, and who have made a careful study of the best preserved of these "rock cities" of Bashan, tell us that everything about them is of stone-doors, gates, windows, stairs, rafters, galleries, cupboards, benches, and even candlesticks. So perfectly preserved are some of these "dead cities," that of one, Salcah, Doctor Porter says that some five hundred of the houses are still standing, and that "from three hundred to four hundred families might settle in it at any moment without laying a stone or expending an hour's labor on repairs." Of Beth-gamul another traveler says in part: "The houses were some of them very large, consisting usually of three rooms on the ground floor, and two on the first story, the stairs being formed of large stones built in the house walls, and leading up outside. The doors were, as usual, of stone; sometimes folding doors, and some of them highly ornamental. I wandered about quite alone in the old streets of the town--entered one by one the old houses, went up-stairs, visited the rooms, and, in short, made a careful examination of the whole place; but so perfect was every street, every house, every room, that I almost fancied I was in a dream, wandering alone in this city of the dead, seeing all perfect, yet not hearing a sound." Much of the work in most of these cities is on such a large scale as to indicate that the houses were built by, and intended for a race of giants. When we think of these fortresses of strength defended by their mighty occupants, and remember that they were probably in existence at the time of the exodus of the Israelites from Egyptian bondage, the victories of Moses gained here become sublime. We are nearing Mezarib. All forenoon has been consumed in covering a distance of only about fifty miles. But by twelve o'clock we have passed almost completely across the land where Og was king, especially that part of his kingdom which, not long after being wrested from him and his giant followers, was assigned to the eastern half-tribe of Manasseh for a permanent possession.

Before leaving Beyrout my dragoman telegraphed to Jerusalem for a muleteer and three horses to be sent to this railroad terminus. Must we be disappointed in this! We are both solicitous. My guide is leaning far out of the car window long before the train stops to learn, if possible, whether or not his order has been obeyed. I watch that dark, anxious, perplexed face with much solicitude. Ah, he smiles! The sunshine of satisfaction chases the clouds of anxiety and doubt from his countenance, and that dark face looks beautiful to me. He is happy, and I share in his happiness. Our muleteer and horses are awaiting us.

"Among Bedouins"
CHAPTER III.

At twelve o'clock our train stopped. I was quickly introduced to him who had been awaiting us, and who was now to join our party--"Haleel," of Jerusalem. He was dressed in typical Eastern fashion, wearing the wide pantaloons, flowing robe, and "kufiyeh"; he was apparently twenty-five years old, dark-skinned, and blind in one eye; he could not speak a word of English; and he was a devout Mohammedan. "Haleel, of Jerusalem!" Notwithstanding his fantastic appearance, the name and place of residence seemed to me a blending of mystery and sacredness. I did not hesitate to extend a cordial greeting, and his smile of confused interest as I tried to shake hands with him while he tried to give me an Oriental salutation won me to him. It was his only intelligible language to me, but it was sufficient to give me assurance of his friendship, and I was beginning to feel that from that hour I should need friends. The salutation that Haleel offered to me was a quick, graceful movement of his hand toward my feet, next to his lips, and then lightly to his forehead. I had seen the natives do this in exchanging salutations, and now that it had been offered to me I sought an interpretation. My guide explained that Haleel meant to tell me that he felt so honored in meeting me, that he "would take the dust from my feet, would kiss it, and then place it on his forehead." Beautiful sentiment! Had I ever previously in my life been so honored in meeting any one!

The greeting over, I noticed unusual movements about the station. Many Turkish soldiers were there. They stood about in groups engaged in animated conversation. Upon inquiry I learned that the feuds so common in that region were again "on," and that the soldiers were there to quell lawlessness. As I was the only tourist there I became an object of special interest. Some of the men came to my dragoman, and only a few words had passed until I knew that I was the subject of their conversation. I could occasionally catch the word "hawadje," which means "master," and I knew they were referring to me. Then they would look at me and shake their heads. I was anxious to know what it all meant, but had to be content with what my guide was pleased to tell of it. He seemed to have gained his point, but he told me nothing except to prepare for a hard trip, as a day's distance must be covered, if possible, before nightfall. As we had already lost two days in Damascus, I was not averse to trying something strenuous in order to make up in part for that loss. I felt quite equal to the task, (though it proved to be a severe ordeal,) when it was explained to me that it would require a ride of more than forty miles to reach a safe halting-place for the night. My guide had planned it; and I was committed to the plan.

After a hurried lunch, eaten in the tent of an Arab, I prepare for,--I know not what. I put on my leggings and head-gear. Then I give over my luggage, which consists of a suit-case, hand-grip, umbrella, and alpenstock, to Haleel. I keep my overcoat, not because the weather is cold,--it is hot,--but because I think I may possibly need it as a kind of cushion for my saddle before the day is over. The need was felt, and SORELY felt quite early in the afternoon; but most of the time we rode too rapidly for my overcoat to supply the need,--it just would not stay where I had hoped it might serve me well. So it happened that I was destined to experience on that ride such misery as I had scarcely thought one could endure. But, I anticipate.

We are ready. I am anxious to be going. I am delighted when my horse, a beauty, indeed, and of pure Arabian stock, is led up by two dusky sons of the desert. Surely my long trip to Jerusalem will be one of pleasure when I am mounted on such a steed! At half-past twelve o'clock we mount, and, facing to the south, we set off at a brisk pace for Gerasa, (known to the Arabs as Jerash,) where it has been planned that we shall spend the night. Several of the natives accompany us a short distance on foot, one running on either side of my horse and holding to the bridle; but soon, with interesting and graceful salaams, they leave us to pursue our hot and dusty way alone.

There are just three of us, and we proceed in the following order: my dragoman, who is guide and interpreter, leads the way; I follow next after him; bringing up the rear is our muleteer, who takes charge of all luggage, cares for the horses, and especially for,--me. Why should I not be happy? For the first time in my life I have two men engaged to look after my wants. They did their duty well,--were almost painfully attentive at times. But to-day I thank them for their kind severity.

Not having spent more than a few hours on horse-back in the previous ten years, I found, after riding a few miles, that it required more than a beautiful horse to make riding comfortable to an inexperienced rider. But our way led through such a beautiful valley, and on either hand were mountains so suggestive of Bible narrative that there was much in the earlier part of the afternoon to divert my attention from any physical discomfort. Where we were riding there was no road,--simply bridle-paths, and frequently not even a path.

After we had been riding for an hour a young Arab on camel-back joined us. I did not like his searching looks from a face almost hidden in his head-garment. But he stayed with us for a half-hour, and in that time had raced his camel with our horses; then he suddenly turned from us toward the near mountains of Gilead. We met a number of caravans in the earlier part of the afternoon, and I noted that every man that I saw carried a gun, or some sort of sword, or large knife. They were ready for defense, if occasion should arise.

About two o'clock we passed a "memorial heap," or cairn. Some tragedy occurred there, and the custom of the region is that the passer-by places reverently on the pile of rocks already formed an additional stone. Elsewhere I had seen this done when it seemed to me the actor was under the spell of a superstitious fear.

About the middle of the afternoon a soldier, full armed, dashes up to us in a mad gallop, hands a message to my dragoman, and then as rapidly rides back again. I am a little alarmed at this until I learn that he has entrusted a writing to us to be delivered in Jerusalem. A little later I see another soldier leave the group in which he is riding and gallop ahead across the open way to the brow of a hill. There he dismounts, lays down his gun, takes the robe, or blanket, on which he rode, spreads it upon the ground, faces toward Mecca, and prostrates himself in prayer. The prayer over, he dashes down to his party and they are off like the wind.

About four o'clock we passed near a little village, the only place where I saw a house on that long afternoon ride. It is not safe for any one to live outside the villages; hence there are no isolated dwellings in all this region. We did not halt for one moment, but kept pressing steadily on.

After five o'clock the plain was deserted; we saw from that time neither man nor beast. I was cramped and painfully tired, and feeling that if I could but walk for a few minutes it would be quite a relief, I dismounted--quite a difficult thing to do and keep from sprawling upon the ground. But I was no sooner off my horse than Haleel was beside me, and my dragoman, who was at that time nearly a hundred yards ahead of me, rode back and sternly commanded: "You get right back on that horse; this is no time to think of walking; you can do that some other time." Inwardly I resented it; how could I stand it longer! I blamed it on the saddle, then I thought that they must have given me the worst horse of the three. But all this helped nothing. They assisted me again into the saddle. Then my guide delivered a little speech in Arabic to Haleel. I did not then understand it, but shortly after I learned the essence of it; it was, "You keep your eye on him and see that he keeps his horse moving." When I found myself again in the saddle I determined that if I must ride there would be no more trotting of my horse,--I would proceed as gently as possible. But, alas! Haleel had his whip and my dream of controlling my horse was over. After that I kept close to my dragoman. At that time I thought it harsh treatment, but later I understood.

We have reached the limit of level land and are now winding among the eastern foot-hills of the mountains of Gilead. It is the hour of sunset and the great orb of day sinks in sad beauty to me. In the twilight I see here and there half-buried pillars of some famous temple--a temple that surely never stood here. Our horses are wet with sweat; we have not halted for lunch; not a drop of water has been seen; night is coming on with its pale moon casting weird shadows about us; we are alone in a land noted for its lawlessness, and yet we are unarmed. We move on almost in silence. There is silence about us, save for the cry now and then of some night-bird. We see no lights save those above us. My guide seems bewildered and uncertain as to the location of the town we seek. I am faint from weariness, and so cramped that at times it is with difficulty that I keep from falling to the ground. I am now quite solicitous as to our safety and not a little alarmed when our way leads through some rocky, narrow passage suggestive of a lurking-place for men of evil intent. But at last, at half-past nine o'clock, after being in the saddle for nine hours, I am aroused from my stupor by a joyful exclamation from my dragoman. A few dim lights are seen,--IT IS GERASA!

My dragoman continued his exclamations of praise thus, "I thank my God for saving my life once more." I said faintly, "Why such words?" "Well," he said, "all natives are expected to be in their villages by sundown, tourists at their destination earlier. It is the custom of this region that tourists must have an escort of soldiers or Bedouins, even in times of peace; and now THE FEUDS ARE ON; and here we have come alone, at night, unarmed; and I am responsible for these horses--they are not mine--and for your life. The ride may have been hard for you, but the hours of anxiety were more trying to me. I have now done it once, but I'll never again assume such a risk--NOT EVEN FOR A MILLION POUNDS!" I had no response that he heard, but mentally I said, "Never again with ME, Mr. Barakat. NO, NEVER!"

Yet I think I never experienced greater joy on entering my own home than on that night when entering and riding through the crooked, narrow lanes of that miserable village of Gilead.

"At Gerasa"
CHAPTER IV.

Though in the village, and therefore relieved of the feeling of special danger, yet we had much difficulty in securing lodging for the night. Our arrival seemed to disturb the peace of dogdom in what otherwise would have been a quiet resting-place. No people were outside their houses. We picked our way to the nearest light; the occupant of the house would not come out, but showed his face at the window--a hole in the wall about a foot square. My dragoman pleaded for lodging, but in vain. We sought the next house in which there was a light, but neither would the people of that home open to us. We tried several other places, but at all of them we were refused admission. They seemed to look with suspicion upon our visit to the village. But, finally, a good old Mohammedan consented to let us spend the night in his rock hut, and gave us the privilege of putting our horses in his little walled space by the house. Haleel must spend the night in this yard--he always slept with the horses. When my dragoman helps me over the stone door-sill, and we enter the hut, we find that the part allotted to men consists of but one small room, having a floor of earth on which are spread a couple of mats. In this room there is no furniture. Two persons are already asleep on the floor. We do not disturb them.

Not having eaten anything since noon, my dragoman begins at once to prepare a light lunch for us. On a brazier that he finds here he makes a little charcoal fire and quickly brews some of the tea brought from Damascus; into this he squeezes lemon juice; then finding some bread that he had stowed away in his saddle-bags, our lunch is ready. I sit on the floor as comfortable as I can make myself while he is getting supper. The flickering light, the shifting shadows, the strange ones lying asleep, the almost as strange dusky helpers, the sense of dangers just escaped, the whining, wailing, barking dogs, my physical pain--all these things beget within me a strange feeling of loneliness and a longing for home. Again and again I ask myself the question, "Why did you undertake this; why were you not content to go down from Damascus to Galilee and all of West Palestine by the easy way?" But, again and again I say to myself: "You would never have been satisfied had you done so; this is part of the price to be paid for what you wanted; consider what you get in exchange, value received."

But my reverie is cut short by a groan from my dragoman; he sank back trembling and said, "Call Haleel!" Together we worked with him for a half-hour or more until a chill, the result of drinking too much water on reaching the village, had been overcome. I was much alarmed at the possible outcome of his sudden illness, for had he left me thus the situation for me would have been one of extreme perplexity. In my anxiety for him I forgot for the moment my own condition. But now I am again a conscious sufferer. So tired am I that I can scarcely wait until I have sipped a little tea and eaten a little bread before I have removed hat and shoes and am stretched out upon the floor to sleep. The horses seem restless in their stamping; the dogs keep up their barking; the room is dark; I hear the heavy breathing of those about me; a lone star peeps in through the small window; and I try to compose myself for the rest that I so much need. "Is there no balm in Gilead?" Yes. I thought that I was lying down to a night of restlessness and fever, but never on couch of down has my rest been sweeter.

I am awakened at dawn by some one moving about in the room, and I see a man pick up a gun and pass quickly out. The dogs are barking savagely throughout the village. Then I look about me. Imagine my surprise when I discover that I have had five bed-fellows, or rather FLOOR-FELLOWS! There we lay stretched out in all sorts of angles and curves--American, Syrian, Circassian; Christian and Mohammedan--forming a kind of crazy patch-work on the earthen floor. And imagine my supreme disgust when I discover a big, dirty, odorous, unshod human foot, erect on the heel and with toes spread out like a fan, within a few inches of my face! Bah! How was it that I slept! I turn my face to the wall and soon lose thought of the disturbing vision in slumber.

It is quite late when again I wake. The host is sitting on his mat near me fumbling beads and chanting prayers. Without moving I watch him for a while and note that he is also interested in me, and that he now knows that I am awake. I begin an investigation of myself, and find, to my glad surprise, that while I am stiff and sore I feel quite refreshed. I dress myself--a simple matter this morning, simply putting on my shoes--and while my dragoman prepares our breakfast I exercise myself somewhat by walking down to an old Roman bridge spanning the small stream flowing through the village. In this half-hour I get a good general knowledge of the location of the town, its outline, its magnificent ruins, etc. But I am not ready yet for sight-seeing. I prefer to listen to the brook singing its happy way almost hidden among the pink oleanders that grow in such profusion along its sides. The running water, the perfume of the flowers, the flood of sunlight--these are like balm to me after my awful yesterday. Certainly I shall be ready early to study the ruins of this wonderful, mysterious, ancient city.

Breakfast is ready. It consists of boiled eggs, bread, cheese, and tea. Our table is the floor on which we slept. The male members of the house-hold join us as we sit on mats around the simple meal. Our host sends one of the men (a visitor to a Mohammedan home never meets, and frequently never sees a woman) to bring a little of his own bread. It does not look at all tempting to me, but I am told that if I wish to secure my host's friendship I must eat of it. This I do, but only once, and now he would be almost willing to die for me should occasion arise.

After breakfast he shows me some antique coins that he had found, and when my guide explains that I am an American schoolmaster, he manifests exceedingly his delight. He almost pulls me out into his little yard where he had been digging, and where he had unearthed an inscribed cylindrical block of marble about two feet in diameter and four feet in length. The lettering is in Greek. He thinks it must tell of hidden treasure. And so it does to me, but not of the kind for which he is looking. The inscription is partially effaced, but I see enough to conclude that it was likely at one time the pedestal of a statue.

I next proceed to take a further general view of this celebrated locality--celebrated, for here are the most noted ruins east of the Jordan. My first observation is that the present inhabitants, Circassians, are rapidly despoiling the treasures of antiquity found here. They take the rocks and pillars of temples that were once the admiration of a great region and pile them roughly together, forming a small enclosure; then, in many instances, they place poles and brush across the top, throw ground on the brush,--and their houses are ready for occupancy. There is no regularity whatever in the plan of the alleys, or lanes, of the present village. We mount our horses for a further study of these interesting ruins.

Gerasa was one of the chief cities of the Decapolis, (the other nine were Damascus, Hippos, Scythopolis, Dion, Pella, Kanatha, Raphana, Gadara, and Philadelphia,) and was situated twenty miles east of the Jordan on one of the northern tributaries of the Jabbok, and within five miles of the place where the famous "Moabite Stone" was found. Tristam considers it to-day as "PROBABLY THE MOST PERFECT ROMAN CITY LEFT ABOVE GROUND." The present ruins seem to date back to the second century of the Christian era. A Christian bishop from Gerasa attended the Council of Seleucia in 359 A.D., and another that of Chalcedon in 451 A.D. In the thirteenth century this city was in ruins. It was then for five centuries lost to the eyes of the civilized world. In the beginning of the thirteenth century a German traveler visited it; the magnificent ruins of the place amazed him. The same ruins to-day, or some of them, strike the comparatively few visitors with awe at the thought of the riches, the gayety, and the power that once reigned here on the border of the desert.

The walls of the ancient city are plainly traceable, and formed an enclosure about a mile square. Three of its gates are fairly well preserved. On the south side of the city ruins, less than a half mile distant, stands a triumphal arch forty feet high. Between this arch and the city wall are the ruins of a great stone pool and of a circus. The main street lies on the west side of the stream. It was paved; yet shows ruts worn into the stones by chariot wheels; and was lined on each side with a row of rock columns above twenty feet in height, some of which have capitals representing a high degree of artistic skill in their planning and execution. Part of this street was arcaded behind the columns where was the sidewalk. Fronting upon this street were vast temples and baths, which, though fallen, are yet grand in their ruins. All along this way lie great blocks of stone and marble and fallen columns, so numerous that at times our progress is almost barred. But not all of the columns are fallen; more than two hundred yet stand on their original bases. About mid-way along the street it is crossed at right angles by another which is also lined with columns. Farther on toward the south it widens into an oval-shaped forum a hundred yards long, surrounded with Ionic pillars in their original positions.

Just beyond the forum, elevated somewhat, is a large, well-preserved temple; and immediately to the right of the temple is a theater built in the hill-side with seats, stage, and other parts plainly distinguishable. It is easy to sit in one of these empty benches and see, as a shadow out of the past, a lively scene presented on the now deserted stage--the voice of eloquence rings clear out of the dead centuries, the play-house resounds with the applause of the shades that fill the seats about me-- and, then, the curtain of mystery is dispelled by the bright sunlight that floods all the landscape, and I see nothing but ruins everywhere. The play is over. The shades have gone again to their long home.

On a commanding position in the north-west quarter stood temples of vast proportions whose spacious courts, tottering walls, and forsaken altars speak in eloquent terms of a glory long since departed. Evidently this was a populous city, for it possessed two theaters capable of seating many thousands of people. That it was a religious city, and much given to idolatry, its temples and altars declare.

While Josephus speaks of the capture of this city by Alexander Jannaeus, about 85 B.C., we look in vain for a mention of it in the Bible. But some recent investigators, notably Dr. Merrill, (with whom I had the pleasure and honor of conversing,) incline to the opinion that Gerasa was the original Ramoth-gilead. Dr. Merrill gives six arguments in favor of his position, which, after my observations made in the place itself, I feel like accepting.

If this were Ramoth-gilead, then how much of Bible story clusters about the spot! It was a "city of refuge"; and over these hills or up and down this valley rushed the accidental man-slayer to seek refuge within its gates from the blood-thirsty pursuer. Here Ahab was slain (I. Kings 22:34-37), here Ahaziah and Jehoram defeated Hazael (II. Kings 8:28, 29; 9:14), and here Jehu was anointed king of Israel and rode forth in a chariot to execute his terrible commission concerning the house of Ahab (II. Kings 9:4-26).

Gerasa! Beautiful, though in ruins. What glory must once have been thine! But where are the warriors who passed in triumph through thy gates? Where are the builders of thy temples? Where are the the priests who ministered at thy altars? Where are the devotees who bowed at thy shrines? Where are the people who thronged thy theaters and trod thy beautiful streets? The hills over which man walked are still here; the rocks that he quarried, carved, polished, and fitted into place are here; the stone coffin in which he lay down to his last resting-place is here--but where is HE? Gone! gone forever! Surely, how frail is man! How fleeting his glory! As the waters of thy stream flow on to the Sea of Death, so has the tide of life which swept through thy streets passed on to the grave and oblivion.

"Up Into the Mountains"
CHAPTER V.

Passing out over the fallen western wall of Gerasa we are immediately in the ancient cemetery, which extends for a mile, or nearly so, from the city. Many stone sarcophagi, some of which are artistically carved, lie scattered about in almost every conceivable position--some even lying across the tops of others. But these windowless rock-palaces are all empty.

Leaving Gerasa, my way leads in a general direction westward over the mountains of Gilead. The reader must remember that in all this region there is not a road over which a carriage can be driven, save that quite recently a few trips have been made from Mezarib to Gerasa. What are called roads are simply bridle-paths, and, in many cases, the paths are so indistinct that the guide is more likely to take you forward with reference to a general direction than to attempt to lead you by a recognized trail.

The Mountains of Gilead present a rugged appearance, but, in the main, are clothed with vegetation; hence they are beautiful in their majesty. The olive and the prickly oak are abundant. The villages are not numerous, and are situated far up the slopes, or even on the tops of the ridges. These villages are clusters of squalid huts constructed of stone and mud, and can afford no accommodation such as an American might desire. But, in many instances, they occupy sites identified with places and events noted in Bible story.

These mountains were given to Gad in the allotment of Joshua and Eleazar. Surely at that time the prospect must have been much more pleasing than at present, or the Gadites would not have been so anxious to receive this district as a permanent possession. True, even now, a few narrow valleys, or wadies, show signs of great fertility, but the greater part is quite uninviting. Yet to the tourist there is much of interest in this region.

My way to the Jordan lay over these mountains, especially that part known as the Jebel Ajlun. Sometimes it seemed impossible to proceed because of rocks and underbrush. The mountain sides were so steep in some places that we were barely able to climb them; many of the wadies, washed by winter torrents, were next to being impassable; and when our way led along the sides of precipitous slopes I shuddered to think of the consequences of a misstep upon the part of my horse. The course I had chosen through this East-Jordan country was an unusual one (as already noted)--one over which my dragoman had never gone, and one over which, he said, not one in a thousand tourists to Palestine ever asked to go,--a statement corroborated by the United States Consul at Jerusalem, who has written extensively on the trans-Jordanic highlands. This statement was not very encouraging to me, but I had set my heart on reaching the Jordan by this route, so simply said, "Lead on." Several times I feared I had made a serious mistake, but having come thus far I could not go back. After we had passed through the old cemetery our ascent was gradual until we reached the modern village of Suf, three miles northwest of Gerasa. Here we see "two women grinding at the mill." The mill consists of two circular stones about fourteen inches in diameter, the one stone rests upon the other, and the grain to be crushed between them is supplied by one of the women while the other turns the upper stone round and round, thus grinding the meal for the uninviting bread of their less inviting floor-table.

This place has been suggested by Major Condor as the probable site of Mizpah in Gilead. A group of fine stone monuments, in ruins, is yet to be seen here. If this be the location of Mizpah then here is the place where Jacob and Laban made their covenant of lasting peace, and erected the "heap of witness" (Gen. 31:44-52), saying, "The Lord watch between me and thee when we are absent one from another." Then they parted, Laban going back to Mesopotamia and Jacob pressing on with anxious heart toward the near Jabbok and the farther lands of his estranged brother Esau.

Inspired by the covenant at Mizpah, and with a desire to help others to establish covenants of peace, and to accept with cheerful resignation enforced separation from loved ones, a recent writer, Julia A. Baker, has written beautifully the following poem entitled "Mizpah":

Go thou thy way and I go mine;
Apart, yet ever near;
Only a veil hangs thin between
The pathways where we are;
And "God keep watch 'tween thee and me,"
This is my prayer;
He looks thy way, he looketh mine,
And keeps us near.

I know not where thy road may lie,
Or which way mine may be;
If mine will lead through parching sands,
And thine beside the sea;
Yet "God keeps watch 'tween thee and me,"
So, never fear.
He holds thy hand, he claspeth mine,
And keeps us near.

Should wealth and fame perchance be thine,
And my lot lowly be,
Or thou be sad or sorrowful,
And glory be for me;
Yet "God keeps watch 'tween thee and me,"
Both be his care;
One arm 'round thee and one 'round me
Will keep us near.

I'll sigh sometimes to see thy face,
But since this cannot be,
I'll leave thee to the care of Him
Who cares for thee and me.
"I'll keep thee both beneath my wings"--
This comfort dear--

One wing o'er thee and one o'er me;
So we are near.

And tho' our paths be separate,
And thy way be not mine,
Yet coming to the mercy-seat,
My soul will meet with thine;
And "God keep watch 'tween thee and me,"
I'll whisper there;
He blesseth thee, he blesseth me,
And we are near.

If this place were Mizpah, then here Jephthah lived; and here, when he went out to fight against the Ammonites, he made the vow to sacrifice whatsoever should come forth out of the doors of his house to meet him on his return from the battle, if the Lord would only give him the victory. The battle was fought, and Jephthah triumphed. The glad news reached his home; and out from his house rushed his daughter, his only child, with timbrels and with dances, to meet her hero-father, not knowing the nature of his vow made on the eve of the battle. Her presence caused the brave warrior to tremble with horror and rend his clothes when he remembered his vow. The daughter was dismayed--instead of a smile of joy from her father she read her doom in his blanched and contorted face. And somewhere on these hills round about the voice of wailing arose for two months from many maidens because Jephthah must fulfill his rash vow by sacrificing his only child. But he did unto her according to his word; and annually thereafter for a period of four days these hills resounded with the voice of weeping--the weeping of the maidens of Mizpah over the sad fate of Jephthah's daughter. (Judges 11.)

Farther on we ascend a high ridge and then begin our descent into the southern branch of the wady of Ajlun. After winding about for some time among the rocks and brush in the dry bed of this wady we finally halt at Ain Jenneh, a good, strong fountain issuing from under a great rock. We are yet in the upper reaches of the wady and near the present village of Ajlun. Here we lunch and rest an hour.

Some authorities identify this region as the place where was the "wood of

Ephraim." That being true, it is the place where Absalom lost his life. Certain it is, even to-day, that to leave the little path that we are following would mean to become hopelessly entangled in jungles of prickly oak and other growth. Even in the path it is with difficulty that I keep my garments from being torn from me.

If this be the location of the "wood of Ephraim," then here the forces of Absalom under Amasa and the armies of David under Joab fought in those trying days of David's exile. Only a few miles away, at Mahanaim, David sent out his men, commanding that they touch not the young man. Then he waited for the news of the conflict. In the thickets of Gilead the first "battle of the wilderness" was fought. It was a decisive engagement. Joab's veterans of many wars were too strong for the rebel's army. Absalom sought safety in flight, but in trying to ride hurriedly through the wild tangle his head caught in the branches of a great oak, and before he could extricate himself, Joab had found him and thrust him through the heart; then Joab's ten armor-bearers encompassed the unfortunate victim and finished the deadly work. And then, though Absalom had reared for himself a beautiful monument in the king's dale at Jerusalem, they took his body from the tree and threw it into a pit near by and made a great heap of stones over it. There was no weeping at the grave of Absalom.

With the death of Absalom the rebellion was at an end; but David's heart was broken. He waited at the gate of the city, more interested in the welfare of his son than in the success of his army. Swift runners approach! In answer to his question, "Is the young man safe?" he hears reply that pierces his heart like a dagger. Up to his chamber over the gate the king slowly passed weeping and bent with grief, and as he went he said, "O my son Absalom! my son, my son Absalom! Would God I had died for thee, O Absalom, my son, my son!"

A poet's conception of David's great grief on hearing of the death of his son is portrayed in the following lines of N. P. Willis:

Alas! my noble boy! that thou shouldst die!
Thou, who wert made so beautifully fair!
That Death should settle in thy glorious eye,
And leave his stillness in thy clustering hair!
How could he mark thee for the silent tomb?

My proud boy, Absalom!

Cold is thy brow, my son! and I am chill,
As to my bosom I have tried to press thee
How was I wont to feel my pulses thrill,

Like a rich harp-string, yearning to caress thee,
And hear thy sweet "MY FATHER!" from these dumb
And cold lips, Absalom!

But death is on thee. I shall hear the gush
Of music, and the voices of the young;
And life will pass me in the mantling blush,
And the dark tresses to the soft winds flung;
But thou no more, with thy sweet voice, shalt come
To meet me, Absalom!

And oh! when I am stricken, and my heart,
Like a bruised reed, is waiting to be broken.
How will its love for thee, as I depart,
Yearn for thine ear to drink its last deep token!
It were so sweet, amid death's gathering gloom,
To see thee, Absalom!

And now, farewell! 'Tis hard to give thee up
With death so like a gentle slumber on thee--
And thy dark sin! Oh! I could drink the cup,
If from this woe its bitterness had won thee.
May God have called thee, like a wanderer, home,
My lost boy, Absalom!

But this fountain! What birds and beasts here drank undisturbed before man came to assert his lordship! What multitudes of people here have drunk from the days before Israel down to the present time--the hunter, the tiller of the soil, the grape-gatherer, the shepherd with his flocks, the warrior and his chief,--all rejoiced and rested here, and were refreshed and strengthened by the water.

Almost with reverence we drink again; then we remount our horses and proceed along the wady past the village of Ajlun where an Arab joins us and guides us on over fertile patches of ground and through olive groves until we reach the modern town of Coefrinje, a town that probably contains several thousand inhabitants. It is in the midst of an olive grove well up on the side of the mountains. Here, although it is scarcely past the middle of the afternoon, we stop for the night. It is too far to the next village to risk going ahead--the way is none too safe, even by day.

Several times to-day I could clearly distinguish the remains of old Roman roads, well paved, and with curbing arrangement excellently preserved. What vast sums of money and what great amount of labor must have been expended on these old high-ways of the time when this territory was occupied by the Romans! And where Rome walked she left her path well made, and she left the impress of her thought in rock-paved road, or in the lasting marble of her pillared temples and carven tombs.

"By the Watch-Tower"
CHAPTER VI.

Soon after entering the village of Coefrinje my dragoman had the rare good fortune to find a former acquaintance, but whom he did not know to be in those mountains. His name was Elias Mitry, who, with his wife, had come up from Jerusalem to do missionary work under the auspices of the Church of England. Although he was a native of Palestine and talked very poor English, yet he offered us a welcome to his humble home than which no more royal was accorded us anywhere. The meeting with my dragoman was an exhibition of genuine joy, and he seemed equally pleased to have me in his home; especially did he consider it an honor to be my host when my dragoman told him that he was escorting a "school-master" through the land. In that land it seems that the teacher is almost reverenced because of his profession, while, it may be said by way of contrast, in some sections of my home land he is scarcely respected because of his profession. Indeed, I was treated as a guest of honor; the best that the home afforded was at my service. Stuffed cucumbers, figs, olives, pomegranates, and what, for want of a better name, I call "congealed grape-juice,"--all these were placed before me when in the early evening they aided my guide in serving supper.

We spent little over four hours in the saddle to-day, so I am not wearied, and I can give interested attention to the surroundings. And there is much to interest me here. For, while the name "Coefrinje" is not mentioned in the Bible, nor is its site definitely identified with the location of any biblical city, yet there is much of Bible story centered at points within five miles of this town.

Just across the narrow valley, only a few hundred yards distant, is the height, Kulat er Rubad. It is crowned with the ruins of an old castle-fortress called (together with the peak on which it stands) the "watch-tower of Gilead." The view from the dismantled ramparts is not excelled in this part of the world. It, indeed, rivals the view from the celebrated peak south of the Jabbok, Jebel Osha. Dr. Thomson says, "In reality this prospect includes more points of biblical and historical interest than any other on the face of the earth." And Dr. Merrill, after enumerating many of the famous characters of history that moved under the gaze of this mount of out-look, adds, "The view is more than a picture. It is a panorama of great variety, beauty, and significance." To me it is wonderfully impressive.

As the evening wore on I first gave attention to the large olive-press close to the mission-house. The press was simple in construction, consisting of a large bowl-shaped rock from the center of whose depression rose an upright post of wood; to this post was fastened a long nearly-horizontal beam, not unlike what might be seen in the old-time cider-mill or cane-mill; slipped onto this beam by means of a large hole in its center was a large stone shaped like a grind-stone; this rock, pushed well up to the post, rested in the bowl of the other rock. When the natives pushed or pulled the beam around in tread-mill fashion the circular stone turned on the beam, and at the same time moved round and round in the hollow of the other rock. Thus the olives placed in the bowl-shaped rock were thoroughly crushed and the oil was caught in vessels.

Then I watch the shepherds leading their large flocks of sheep and goats in from the mountain pastures to their folds for the night. All day these faithful guardians have been with their flocks seeking good pasture and water for them,--no easy task in the fall of the year near the end of the dry season. They have guarded the sheep from the danger of beast, or precipice, or pit; have released those caught in the under-brush; have ministered to the needs of the sick; and now as night approaches they come leading--not driving--their flocks in quiet movement from out the mountain-paths to the sheltering fold in the village for the night, again to lead them forth on to-morrow, and to do likewise day after day. To see the tender solicitude of the Oriental shepherd for his sheep adds much to one's appreciation of the beauty and fitness of the teaching of the Master in his parable of the Good Shepherd.

But it is near the sunset hour of my only evening in these sacred mountains. I seek a vantage-ground and watch the King of Day sink slowly down to his couch of rest behind the western mountains and the farther sea. Oh, how beautiful! The sky is ablaze with a glory indescribable by mortal tongue. All space seems vocal with praise to the God of love and beauty.

In the strange and peaceful quiet of that evening I felt the presence of a mysterious, subtle influence stirring within me. In the shower of gold flung out as a good-night to me, and as the star of evening smiled down upon me in the purpling twilight and began calling her myriads of companions to their sentry-posts to keep watch over me through the hours of the night in that strange land, I felt, I think, the spirit of the poetry,

"Sunset and evening star,
And one clear call for me," etc.,

in its fullness. Indeed, the air seemed vibrant with a living personality, which, without undue stretching of the imagination, I recognized as the SPIRIT OF HISTORY come to tell me the wonderful story of those wonderful mountains. Enraptured I listened.

SAID THE SPIRIT: "Long before Gad was attracted by these heights and valleys, tribes of people lived here in their simplicity, yet in sin. The land seemed not different from other lands. Here were towering wooded mountain, rocky ravine, and strong-flowing fountain; here the beast prowled among the rocks, the bird nested in the trees, and the sweet-scented flowers graced all the landscape. The storms beat upon the mountains and the waters rushed in madness to the valley in the rainy season, and the sun scorched the vegetation and dried up the fountains in the dry season. Thus in monotony centuries passed.

"But one day the God of heaven sent messengers to encamp here, and from that time these mountains on which you now stand have been considered sacred-- because pressed by the feet of angels. Yonder to the northeast, only a little way, is where that event took place. Jacob, rich in herds and flocks, was on his way home from far-off Euphrates, but he was much troubled at the thought of meeting his brother who had sought to take his life about twenty years previously. He was picking his way slowly over these mountains leading his company and cattle when there appeared in his way a host of angels. He was not frightened, but in gladness of heart he cried out, 'Mahanaim,'--God's host. And although the wise people of your day are not quite sure as to the exact location of this meeting, yet be happy in the thought that you are now only a few miles from the sacred spot, if, indeed, you are not just where it occurred. Had you then stood here you could have seen the glorious light of their presence, and could almost have heard the rustle of their heaven-plumed pinions.

"After this meeting Jacob wandered a little farther to the south, and just over yonder, on the Jabbok, he spent a whole night in prayer and in wrestling with the Angel Jehovah, thinking it was a mere man. There he gained a great victory over self, and he received the new name, 'Israel.' And on the next day, a little farther to the south, he met his erst-while angry and murderous brother in peace and happy reconciliation.

"A few centuries pass. Then the mighty Moses conquers all this region; and a little later these Ajlun Mountains were given to the tribe of Gad as a permanent home. But, in the course of time, the native tribes prove troublesome; and then the great Gideon, having gained a decisive victory down in the valley, followed the fleeing enemy, 'faint, yet pursuing,' right through this very district. Later the Ammonites were punished in a great battle by Israel's 'out-cast,' and mighty warrior, Jephthah.

"But look again at Mahanaim where Jacob met the angels. The place in later centuries became a center of other events of interest. There, after the death of Saul, Ish-bosheth established his capital, and forth from its gates he sent his armies under Abner to fight that he might secure the scepter of all Israel to himself. But after two years of struggle he was treacherously slain and his cause was hopelessly lost. There, too, David sought refuge from Absalom; and out from those same gates through which Ish-bosheth had sent armies against him, David sent armies against his own son. And there above one of the gates of Mahanaim the voice of his weeping arose when he heard the news of the death of his strange misguided boy.

"Time passed on and the Israelites turned from the God of heaven to worship at the shrines of other gods. Then, to punish them for their sin God sent a strange invader into these mountains who carried away the people by thousands into cruel captivity in a land far toward the sun-rising.

"Later the Romans came and planted olive trees and built fine cities and established enduring roads. But Rome is fallen, and where she moved in power and splendor ruin only remains, and the unambitious, ignorant Bedouin feeds his flock and lives in idleness amidst broken down terraces and thorn-covered fertile soil. Desolate! Yes, dark is the picture. But, what of the night? Take your place again on the 'watch-tower of Gilead' and scan well the horizon. Yes, it is well; the morning cometh!"

Having given myself up to reverie and to communing with the SPIRIT OF HIS-TORY, as it were, I was for a time forgetful of my surroundings. The twilight had deepened when I again turned my thoughts to the village and its people. I look up at some of the houses near me and see a number of the natives in their dark robes standing like statues on the flat roofs of their homes, yet watching every movement of the stranger that has so unexpectedly appeared in their midst. I do not fear them, but somehow a feeling of unrest steals over me; they seem like shades of departed Israelites back again from their long sleep. In the gathering gloom I pass quickly into the mission-house near by.

This proves to be an evening full of interest to me. I learn that a mission-service is soon to begin, and that a number of the villagers will be here for the service. I am impressed with the quiet (save for the barking of dogs) that prevails in these Arab villages. I see no drunkenness, and there is no boisterous rudeness of other sort.

In a little while a score or more of men come quietly to the mission-house, remove their sandals, pass into the room, and seat themselves on the earthen floor against the walls. Mrs. Mitry beckons to me to come to the door; she wanted me to see that row of forty sandals. She said in her broken way that it was interesting to her, and she thought it would interest me.

It is only a little while until Mr. Mitry enters and takes his place at a small table in the center of the room. A half hour or more is spent in smoking cigarettes--almost every native smokes. Here it seems that the habit is in no sense considered a vice. Indeed, the missionary himself, not only smokes, but assists in making cigarettes for the others. They smoke and smoke until the room is so darkened that we see each other but dimly through the haze. I am surprised that I can endure it. The tobacco must be different from that used in America, for ordinarily a single cigarette is more offensive to me than was the smoke of nearly fifty on that evening--for some of the men smoked two or three apiece in that close room.

After the smoking was over black coffee was served in small cups holding about one-fourth as much as the average teacup. They sip this slowly and talk. I note that frequently they are saying something about "hawadje," and then they fix their eyes upon me. My dragoman tells me that he has been explaining our hard trip to Gerasa, that they were skeptical about it, but that he has convinced them of its verity.

But now it is time for the service. Mr. Mitry opens his Bible and reads in Arabic the story of Moses' invitation to Hobab. Then he expounds the Scripture for some time while the men listen with rapt attention. There are some questions and answers. I understand only a word now and then, but it is a picture of more than ordinary interest to me to look upon the expectant, and then the satisfied faces of these natives.

When the lesson was over a request came from the men for me to speak to them. Through my dragoman as interpreter I spoke a little while on the theme of the evening, which meant much to me there where the migration of Moses was in a measure felt by the early inhabitants. They listened attentively, and when I had finished they told my guide to say to "hawadje" that they wanted him to stay and make his home with them. Then, the meeting over, they moved out into the darkness with graceful "salaams," and with the promise of one of their number to accompany us on the morrow. They said we must not go on alone.

The service-room is now to be my bed-room. A pallet is brought to me, and on it I am soon trying to sleep. But the beautiful sunset, the vision of the past of this region, the mission-service, the stillness of the night--so still that the very silence seems audible--keep me awake for some time. I am lying by the "watch-tower of Gilead." I seem to see the Spirit of Prophecy standing on its broken battlements, wrapped in the shadows of the night, looking hopefully toward the place of sunrising. I call to him, "Watchman, what of the night?" In sweet tones of assurance comes the answer, "The morning cometh! The story of the Christ will yet transform the darkness that rests here into the brightness of noonday." Then a sweet peace seemed wafted into my soul from out the unseen somewhere,--but certainly from Him who "giveth his beloved sleep."

"Down to the Jordan"
CHAPTER VII.

It was early on the following morning when our horses were led around to the door of the mission-house, but notwithstanding the early hour a dozen or more of the natives were standing in line to receive medical attention from the missionary. A few were there who seemed to have come to witness our departure. Our guide, promised the night before, was on hand, mounted, ready to lead the way over what proved to be by far the roughest part of my trip. For that day my party consisted of four persons. Our new leader, whose name I did not learn, was a man of about fifty years, and was a genuine Arab in appearance and dress. But he wore nothing on his feet--not even sandals. I felt better satisfied, knowing that he would lead the way on that day, for my dragoman was not familiar with that part of Gilead. However, when toward the middle of the afternoon we descended into the Jordan Valley, he was quite at home again.

Single file we proceed from Coefrinje along a narrow path with the bushes and briars brushing the sides of our horses and wetting us with dew. It is not long until we begin to ascend a high ridge. Here there are no paths whatever, and at times our horses can scarcely move on because of the steepness of the ascent. But a few minutes before nine o'clock, after a toilsome struggle, we reach the summit of the ridge, and here I get my first panoramic view of the west-Jordan country. It is entrancingly beautiful.

When we had reined up our horses I said to my dragoman, "Tell our attendants to be still until I have finished speaking; I want to explain the scene before us." And then while he listened, and looked as I directed, I said: "That towering height far to the north is Mount Hermon; the sheet of water some miles on this side is the Sea of Galilee; to the west of the Sea of Galilee is Hattin, the Mount of Beatitudes; that white spot southwest of Hattin is Nazareth; that great plain south of Nazareth is Es-draelon, the 'battle-field of Palestine'; these rounded mountains here in the eastern part of the Valley of Esdraelon are Tabor, Little Hermon, and Gilboa;--on the north is Tabor, at whose base Napoleon fought; the next is Little Hermon, where lived the witch of Endor; and the one south of Little Hermon is Gilboa, where Saul and his sons were slain; that range of mountains forming the southern wall of Esdraelon is Carmel, where Elijah held his trial with the priests of Baal; here below us, winding in its serpentine course, is the Jordan in its great trough or Ghor; in the center of the picture are the mountains of Samaria, with Ebal and Gerizim; to the south are the mountains of Judea, where lies Jerusalem; and that broad expanse of water beyond all these is the Mediterranean, the 'great sea toward the going down of the sun.'"

Then I waited for his criticism. He said, "You are right in every point, but how did you know?" I said, "It is just like the Palestine of my childhood's fancy that I located in the field back of the barn on my father's little farm in western Pennsylvania, and with that picture I have been familiar from the days of my early youth." It is impossible for me to express what were my feelings at this supreme moment of my life, as I viewed for the first time what is distinctively known as the land of Patriarch, Prophet, Priest, and King--the land of my Redeemer's earthly pilgrimage--the world's best Holy Land! After some time spent in viewing that al-most matchless scene, and in gathering mountain lilies, we began our descent into the most remarkable depression in the world--the great Ghor of the Jordan. The next few hours afforded little of pleasure. Careful attention had to be given to our horses as we wound about among the rocks. The horses of both my dragoman and muleteer fell on this trip, but without serious results to either horses or riders. It was quite wearying to proceed thus, so when we finally reached a large sloping rock under which was a kind of stagnant pool--the only water we had seen since leaving Coefrinje--I was glad to know that there we would lunch, even though I could not drink of the water.

This rocky wady is like a prison-house to me. But while eating I hear sweet strains of music somewhere on the mountains--it is from a shepherd's pipe. Scan-ning the heights I see far above me shepherds with their flocks of sheep and goats, and the music that I hear is from their reed-harps which they play as they lead the way over rugged mountain paths to find greener pastures and better waters.

We tarry here only a little while. Not long after lunch we pass a grotto of small size in the hill-side. Evidently the carven ruins are the remains of an ancient temple that stood here in the days when a pagan people held possession of the land; and I feel sure that a fountain must exist here a good part of the year, though now it is dry.

A little farther on is Jabesh-gilead. The story of Jabesh-gilead is a touching one. The people of the city were besieged by the Ammonites under their king, Nahash. The men of the city were willing to make a covenant to serve the Ammonites. But Nahash told them that the only condition on which he would make a covenant with them would be to thrust out all their right eyes and lay it as a reproach upon Israel. The elders of Jabesh asked a respite of seven days in which to get help, which request was granted. The situation was critical in the extreme. Messengers left the besieged city and hurried to the new king of Israel. Saul heard the story of their distresses. Immediately he gathered an army of three hundred and thirty thousand men, and, marching rapidly up the Jordan Valley, crossed the river and attacked the Ammonites and completely routed them with great slaughter. And thus he saved the city.

The men of Jabesh-gilead never forgot Saul and his kindness to them. Forty years later the disastrous battle of Gilboa was fought. In this battle both Saul and Jonathan were slain. The next day when the Philistines searched for spoils among the dead they found Saul and his three sons, and they cut off his head to carry it as a trophy to Philistia; but they took the headless trunks of the king and his sons to Beth-shan and fastened them against its walls as a terrible warning to the Israelites. But, "when the inhabitants of Jabesh-gilead heard of that which the Philistines had done to Saul, all the valiant men arose and went all night and took the body of Saul and the bodies of his sons from the wall of Bethshan and came to Jabesh and burnt them there. And they took their bones and buried them under a tree at Jabesh, and fasted seven days." (II. Samuel 31:11-13.)

Off to the left a little way I see Tabakat Fahil, identified as Pella, the place to which the Christians of Jerusalem fled just before the siege of Titus in obedience to the prophetic warning of Christ.

It is two o'clock when we reach the Jordan Valley, at a point a little south of Beth-shan, which is on the west side of the river. We now turn northward and pursue our way steadily near the mountains until after five o'clock; then we turn toward the river, which we reach at sun-down.

The Jordan Valley is covered with a growth of thorn said to be like that used in the crowning of Christ at the time of his mock-trial. We eat of a delicious yellow berry now ripening on these thorns. We pass two or three small villages, the names of which I could not learn. We cross a number of small streams this afternoon, the largest of which is the Tayibeh. All of these streams are thickly lined with reeds and pink oleander; so thick is this growth in some places that the streams are completely hidden. Our Arab guide springs down into each of these water-brooks and hands drink to us, but he drinks, I think, after the manner of the drinking of "Gideon's three hundred," in the time of their being tested; that is, by a quick movement of the hand throwing water into his mouth.

Pushing rapidly across the open valley we startle gazelles from their hiding-places among the reeds. Then, near the river, we pass several encampments of Bedouins whose tents are black as those of Kedar. At last, after being in the saddle all of ten hours, just at sun-set, we reach the Jordan at the bridge of Jisr el Mejamia, six miles south of the Sea of Galilee. Just across on the other side of the river we shall tarry through the night.

The way has been long and trying. I am very weary. But, now, just before me the Jordan--sacred stream! And then, on the other side, rest! Happy, soul-cheering thought!

"At the Bridge"
CHAPTER VIII.

The bridge of Jisr el Mejamia was at the time of my visit the only available one for travel between the Sea of Galilee and the Dead Sea. It is a stone bridge and was built by the Romans nearly, or quite, two thousand years ago. It could scarcely be crossed by carriages at present as the ascent to the highest point is by a kind of step arrangement. It even seemed a wise precaution for us not to attempt to ride over on horse-back--the stones were very smooth and slippery. The present name of the structure means "bridge of the messengers," and it was so named because here messengers from various points in the land used to meet to exchange messages.

I am glad to reach this place, for again I am very tired. The distance traveled to-day is said to be fifty miles. But when we arrive here the road and bridge are crowded with sheep and goats being brought in from the valley for safety in the night. My first sight of the Jordan, which at this place is clear and sparkling, does not particularly impress me. I long for rest, and so we do not tarry, but pass directly into the village lying just at the west end of the bridge.

Oh, the wretchedness of this place! I wonder what kind of entertainment I can find here. There is little choice as to a place of lodging. The best and only accommodation that the miserable village affords is what was formerly used by robbers as a prison-house for their victims, but which is now used as a kind of store-room. There is but one room, and its earthen floor is littered over with filth of almost every description, while dust and cob-webs everywhere abound. This is the RECEPTION-ROOM for our party of four.

While my dragoman busied himself in getting supper, I sat on a box making notes of what I had seen and experienced that day. Just then the place served as

KITCHEN and WRITING-ROOM. I wrote rapidly, and as I wrote the thought that somewhere that day I had crossed the path of the Master in his Perean ministry thrilled me. I said, "Mr. Barakat, I am going down to the Jordan for a while after supper." He replied, "All right, and I'll go with you'." "No," said I, "I want to be alone down at the bridge." He simply said, "I'll go with you."

Our supper was a light affair, but our host brought a platter of something that looked like dark beeswax, but which proved to be a palatable food called "halawa." We ate from the floor of this room, which then became our DINING-ROOM.

After supper I was ready to go down to the river, not more than a hundred yards from our lodging-place. When we started, our host stepped to a corner of the room, picked up a gun, and prepared to go with us. I told my dragoman to tell him not to go with us. The reply was, "He will go with us." "Well," I said, "if he must go make him put down that gun; it will spoil my evening of quiet thought at the sacred river." The answer was: "Make no further objection. Have you not noticed that everybody here carries a gun? He knows what he is doing. This is the most disreputable place along the river. Those Bedouins of the black tents that we passed over yonder would want no better opportunity than to find you, who are expected to have money, alone at the bridge." I accepted the situation, and said, "All right, but I shall expect you both to be obedient to the extent of giving me a period of quiet as long as I wish to remain."

But, before we go to the bridge, let me tell of that night in that miserable place of filth. At the time of retiring my host said to me through my interpreter that I could have choice of beds--that I could either sleep on the counter, which consisted of a couple of boards laid carelessly across boxes, or that I could sleep behind the counter on the floor! After looking at the boards, and thinking what would likely be the result should I attempt to sleep there, I made choice of the floor. The room then became my BEDROOM.

Oh, that night! I did not sleep a half-hour. The place seemed alive with vermin. My host slept on the counter. He did not seem to be annoyed in the least. True, he scratched, but he snored an accompaniment to his scratching throughout the night. I could only scratch and listen to him; there was no snoring for me. After that night it required frequent bathing and much searching for a week or ten days before I felt free from the awful pests of that filthy den. Thus it was that my first crossing of the

Jordan did not bring me to a "land of rest," but to an experience akin to distraction.

But now to the bridge. We pass quietly among the curious gazers down to the river. Just south of the bridge I go down to the river's edge and bathe my hands, face, and feet in water that only a few hours ago was in the lake where the waves were once stilled by His quiet command of power--"Peace, be still," and where He at another time walked amidst the billows to meet his own; in water that will hurry on down the valley to the place where He was baptized; and then it will pass on into oblivion in the Salt Sea of Death. Then I try, with surprising success, to drink of the water like our Arab guide drank to-day. Then we walk to the bridge, at the approach of which I ask my men to tarry while I go out on it alone to meditate.

I have reached this place by the expenditure of much physical energy. I am very weary over my hard day in the saddle. But when I seat myself on the highest point of the bridge, and give myself up to reverie, I feel the flood of sentiment and rejoice. The moon is about one-half hour above the mountains of Gilead; a halo seems to gild the heights to the east and to the west. I am just above the Jordan; its rippling waters tell me of Abraham, of Jacob, of Joshua, of Saul, of David, of Elijah, of Elisha, of Naaman, of John the Baptist, and of Jesus of Nazareth. How sweet and musical is the story! How impressive its truths as I hear it to-night? Then I watch the play of the moon-light on the water,--the glittering sheen on the smooth surface above the bridge, and the flashes of light on the rapids below. It is all so beautiful!

And this is the Jordan! For many years I have heard of it; I have read of it; I have sung of it. It has been to me for many years a type of death. Again I look upon the calm blue depths on the north, and then again on the rapids below--I see the peace here, and hear the rush there. Then I turn my eyes again to the mountains, and upward to the moon, and past the moon to the stars--and by faith beyond the stars to search for Him of this land, because of whose earth-life I am here, and upon whom I rely for support in the hour of my approach to the shore of that river of which this is the type.

The Codes Of Hammurabi And Moses
W. W. Davies

The discovery of the Hammurabi Code is one of the greatest achievements of archaeology, and is of paramount interest, not only to the student of the Bible, but also to all those interested in ancient history...

Religion   **ISBN:** *1-59462-338-4*

Pages:132
MSRP $12.95

QTY

The Theory of Moral Sentiments
Adam Smith

This work from 1749. contains original theories of conscience amd moral judgment and it is the foundation for systemof morals.

Philosophy   **ISBN:** *1-59462-777-0*

Pages:536
MSRP $19.95

QTY

Jessica's First Prayer
Hesba Stretton

In a screened and secluded corner of one of the many railway-bridges which span the streets of London there could be seen a few years ago, from five o'clock every morning until half past eight, a tidily set-out coffee-stall, consisting of a trestle and board, upon which stood two large tin cans, with a small fire of charcoal burning under each so as to keep the coffee boiling during the early hours of the morning when the work-people were thronging into the city on their way to their daily toil...

Childrens   **ISBN:** *1-59462-373-2*

Pages:84
MSRP $9.95

QTY

My Life and Work
Henry Ford

Henry Ford revolutionized the world with his implementation of mass production for the Model T automobile. Gain valuable business insight into his life and work with his own auto-biography... "We have only started on our development of our country we have not as yet, with all our talk of wonderful progress, done more than scratch the surface. The progress has been wonderful enough but..."

Biographies/ **ISBN:** *1-59462-198-5*

Pages:300
MSRP $21.95

QTY

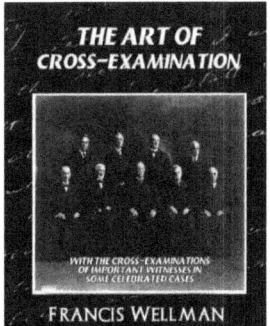

QTY

The Art of Cross-Examination
Francis Wellman

I presume it is the experience of every author, after his first book is published upon an important subject, to be almost overwhelmed with a wealth of ideas and illustrations which could readily have been included in his book, and which to his own mind, at least, seem to make a second edition inevitable. Such certainly was the case with me; and when the first edition had reached its sixth impression in five months, I rejoiced to learn that it seemed to my publishers that the book had met with a sufficiently favorable reception to justify a second and considerably enlarged edition. ..

Pages:412

Reference   ISBN: *1-59462-647-2*   *MSRP $19.95*

QTY

On the Duty of Civil Disobedience
Henry David Thoreau

Thoreau wrote his famous essay, On the Duty of Civil Disobedience, as a protest against an unjust but popular war and the immoral but popular institution of slave-owning. He did more than write—he declined to pay his taxes, and was hauled off to gaol in consequence. Who can say how much this refusal of his hastened the end of the war and of slavery ?

Law   ISBN: *1-59462-747-9*   **Pages:48**

MSRP $7.45

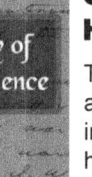

QTY

Dream Psychology Psychoanalysis for Beginners
Sigmund Freud

Sigmund Freud, born Sigismund Schlomo Freud (May 6, 1856 - September 23, 1939), was a Jewish-Austrian neurologist and psychiatrist who co-founded the psychoanalytic school of psychology. Freud is best known for his theories of the unconscious mind, especially involving the mechanism of repression; his redefinition of sexual desire as mobile and directed towards a wide variety of objects; and his therapeutic techniques, especially his understanding of transference in the therapeutic relationship and the presumed value of dreams as sources of insight into unconscious desires.

Pages:196

Psychology   ISBN: *1-59462-905-6*   *MSRP $15.45*

QTY

The Miracle of Right Thought
Orison Swett Marden

Believe with all of your heart that you will do what you were made to do. When the mind has once formed the habit of holding cheerful, happy, prosperous pictures, it will not be easy to form the opposite habit. It does not matter how improbable or how far away this realization may see, or how dark the prospects may be, if we visualize them as best we can, as vividly as possible, hold tenaciously to them and vigorously struggle to attain them, they will gradually become actualized, realized in the life. But a desire, a longing without endeavor, a yearning abandoned or held indifferently will vanish without realization.

Pages:360

Self Help   ISBN: *1-59462-644-8*   *MSRP $25.45*

www.bookjungle.com *email: sales@bookjungle.com fax: 630-214-0564 mail: Book Jungle PO Box 2226 Champaign, IL 61825*

QTY

The Rosicrucian Cosmo-Conception Mystic Christianity *by Max Heindel*   ISBN: *1-59462-188-8*   **$38.95**
The Rosicrucian Cosmo-conception is not dogmatic, neither does it appeal to any other authority than the reason of the student. It is: not controversial, but is: sent forth in the, hope that it may help to clear...   New Age/Religion Pages 646

Abandonment To Divine Providence *by Jean-Pierre de Caussade*   ISBN: *1-59462-228-0*   **$25.95**
"The Rev. Jean Pierre de Caussade was one of the most remarkable spiritual writers of the Society of Jesus in France in the 18th Century. His death took place at Toulouse in 1751. His works have gone through many editions and have been republished...   Inspirational/Religion Pages 400

Mental Chemistry *by Charles Haanel*   ISBN: *1-59462-192-6*   **$23.95**
Mental Chemistry allows the change of material conditions by combining and appropriately utilizing the power of the mind. Much like applied chemistry creates something new and unique out of careful combinations of chemicals the mastery of mental chemistry...   New Age/Business Pages 354

The Letters of Robert Browning and Elizabeth Barret Barrett 1845-1846 vol II   ISBN: *1-59462-193-4*   **$35.95**
by Robert Browning and Elizabeth Barrett   Biographies Pages 596

Gleanings In Genesis (volume I) *by Arthur W. Pink*   ISBN: *1-59462-130-6*   **$27.45**
Appropriately has Genesis been termed "the seed plot of the Bible" for in it we have, in germ form, almost all of the great doctrines which are afterwards fully developed in the books of Scripture which follow...   Religion/Inspirational Pages 420

The Master Key *by L. W. de Laurence*   ISBN: *1-59462-001-6*   **$30.95**
In no branch of human knowledge has there been a more lively increase of the spirit of research during the past few years than in the study of Psychology, Concentration and Mental Discipline. The requests for authentic lessons in Thought Control, Mental Discipline and...   New Age/Business Pages 422

The Lesser Key Of Solomon Goetia *by L. W. de Laurence*   ISBN: *1-59462-092-X*   **$9.95**
This translation of the first book of the "Lemegton" which is now for the first time made accessible to students of Talismanic Magic was done, after careful collation and edition, from numerous Ancient Manuscripts in Hebrew, Latin, and French...   New Age/Occult Pages 92

Rubaiyat Of Omar Khayyam *by Edward Fitzgerald*   ISBN:*1-59462-332-5*   **$13.95**
Edward Fitzgerald, whom the world has already learned, in spite of his own efforts to remain within the shadow of anonymity, to look upon as one of the rarest poets of the century, was born at Bredfield, in Suffolk, on the 31st of March, 1809. He was the third son of John Purcell...   Music Pages 172

Ancient Law *by Henry Maine*   ISBN: *1-59462-128-4*   **$29.95**
The chief object of the following pages is to indicate some of the earliest ideas of mankind, as they are reflected in Ancient Law, and to point out the relation of those ideas to modern thought.   Religion/History Pages 452

Far-Away Stories *by William J. Locke*   ISBN: *1-59462-129-2*   **$19.45**
"Good wine needs no bush, but a collection of mixed vintages does. And this book is just such a collection. Some of the stories I do not want to remain buried for ever in the museum files of dead magazine-numbers an author's not unpardonable vanity..."   Fiction Pages 272

Life of David Crockett *by David Crockett*   ISBN: *1-59462-250-7*   **$27.45**
"Colonel David Crockett was one of the most remarkable men of the times in which he lived. Born in humble life, but gifted with a strong will, an indomitable courage, and unremitting perseverance...   Biographies/New Age Pages 424

Lip-Reading *by Edward Nitchie*   ISBN: *1-59462-206-X*   **$25.95**
Edward B. Nitchie, founder of the New York School for the Hard of Hearing, now the Nitchie School of Lip-Reading, Inc, wrote "LIP-READING Principles and Practice". The development and perfecting of this meritorious work on lip-reading was an undertaking...   How-to Pages 400

A Handbook of Suggestive Therapeutics, Applied Hypnotism, Psychic Science   ISBN: *1-59462-214-0*   **$24.95**
by Henry Munro   Health/New Age/Health/Self-help Pages 376

A Doll's House: and Two Other Plays *by Henrik Ibsen*   ISBN: *1-59462-112-8*   **$19.95**
Henrik Ibsen created this classic when in revolutionary 1848 Rome. Introducing some striking concepts in playwriting for the realist genre, this play has been studied the world over.   Fiction/Classics/Plays 308

The Light of Asia *by sir Edwin Arnold*   ISBN: *1-59462-204-3*   **$13.95**
In this poetic masterpiece, Edwin Arnold describes the life and teachings of Buddha. The man who was to become known as Buddha to the world was born as Prince Gautama of India but he rejected the worldly riches and abandoned the reigns of power when...   Religion/History/Biographies Pages 170

The Complete Works of Guy de Maupassant *by Guy de Maupassant*   ISBN: *1-59462-157-8*   **$16.95**
"For days and days, nights and nights, I had dreamed of that first kiss which was to consecrate our engagement, and I knew not on what spot I should put my lips..."   Fiction/Classics Pages 240

The Art of Cross-Examination *by Francis L. Wellman*   ISBN: *1-59462-309-0*   **$26.95**
Written by a renowned trial lawyer, Wellman imparts his experience and uses case studies to explain how to use psychology to extract desired information through questioning.   How-to/Science/Reference Pages 408

Answered or Unanswered? *by Louisa Vaughan*   ISBN: *1-59462-248-5*   **$10.95**
Miracles of Faith in China   Religion Pages 112

The Edinburgh Lectures on Mental Science (1909) *by Thomas*   ISBN: *1-59462-008-3*   **$11.95**
This book contains the substance of a course of lectures recently given by the writer in the Queen Street Hail, Edinburgh. Its purpose is to indicate the Natural Principles governing the relation between Mental Action and Material Conditions...   New Age/Psychology Pages 148

Ayesha *by H. Rider Haggard*   ISBN: *1-59462-301-5*   **$24.95**
Verily and indeed it is the unexpected that happens! Probably if there was one person upon the earth from whom the Editor of this, and of a certain previous history, did not expect to hear again...   Classics Pages 380

Ayala's Angel *by Anthony Trollope*   ISBN: *1-59462-352-X*   **$29.95**
The two girls were both pretty, but Lucy who was twenty-one who supposed to be simple and comparatively unattractive, whereas Ayala was credited, as her Bombwhat romantic name might show, with poetic charm and a taste for romance. Ayala when her father died was nineteen...   Fiction Pages 484

The American Commonwealth *by James Bryce*   ISBN: *1-59462-286-8*   **$34.45**
An interpretation of American democratic political theory. It examines political mechanics and society from the perspective of Scotsman James Bryce   Politics Pages 572

Stories of the Pilgrims *by Margaret P. Pumphrey*   ISBN: *1-59462-116-0*   **$17.95**
This book explores pilgrims religious oppression in England as well as their escape to Holland and eventual crossing to America on the Mayflower, and their early days in New England...   History Pages 268

QTY

The Fasting Cure *by Sinclair Upton*   ISBN: *1-59462-222-1* $13.95

*In the Cosmopolitan Magazine for May, 1910, and in the Contemporary Review (London) for April, 1910, I published an article dealing with my experi-
ences in fasting. I have written a great many magazine articles, but never one which attracted so much attention...   New Age/Self Help/Health Pages 164*

Hebrew Astrology *by Sepharial*   ISBN: *1-59462-308-2* $13.45

*In these days of advanced thinking it is a matter of common observation that we have left many of the old landmarks behind and that we are now pressing
forward to greater heights and to a wider horizon than that which represented the mind-content of our progenitors...   Astrology Pages 144*

Thought Vibration or The Law of Attraction in the Thought World   ISBN: *1-59462-127-6* $12.95

by William Walker Atkinson   Psychology/Religion Pages 144

Optimism *by Helen Keller*   ISBN: *1-59462-108-X* $15.95

*Helen Keller was blind, deaf, and mute since 19 months old, yet famously learned how to overcome these handicaps, communicate with the world, and
spread her lectures promoting optimism. An inspiring read for everyone...   Biographies/Inspirational Pages 84*

Sara Crewe *by Frances Burnett*   ISBN: *1-59462-360-0* $9.45

*In the first place, Miss Minchin lived in London. Her home was a large, dull, tall one, in a large, dull square, where all the houses were alike, and all the
sparrows were alike, and where all the door-knockers made the same heavy sound...   Childrens/Classic Pages 88*

The Autobiography of Benjamin Franklin *by Benjamin Franklin*   ISBN: *1-59462-135-7* $24.95

*The Autobiography of Benjamin Franklin has probably been more extensively read than any other American historical work, and no other book of its kind
has had such ups and downs of fortune. Franklin lived for many years in England, where he was agent...   Biographies/History Pages 332*

Name	
Email	
Telephone	
Address	
City, State ZIP	

☐ **Credit Card**   ☐ **Check / Money Order**

Credit Card Number	
Expiration Date	
Signature	

Please Mail to: Book Jungle
PO Box 2226
Champaign, IL 61825
or Fax to: 630-214-0564

ORDERING INFORMATION

web: *www.bookjungle.com*
email: *sales@bookjungle.com*
fax: *630-214-0564*
mail: *Book Jungle PO Box 2226 Champaign, IL 61825*
or PayPal *to sales@bookjungle.com*

Please contact us for bulk discounts